The Chocolate Train

By Joanne Kornfeld

Illustrations by Barbara Mason Rast

Earthkids Publishing
P.O. Box 1005
Medford, New York 11763
www.earthkidspublishing.com

Copyright 2002
Library of Congress 2002 132976
ISBN 0-9704629-3-X
Printed in China by Regent Publishing Services Limited

Publisher's Cataloguing-in-Publication

(Provided by Quality Books, Inc.)

Kornfeld, Joanne.
   The chocolate train / by Joanne Kornfeld;
 illustrations by Barbara Mason Rast, -- 1st ed,
      p. cm.
   SUMMARY: this fantasy about a locomotive who learns
 what cooperation and friendship really mean includes
 step-by-step recipes for making chocolate and a design
 for a train candy dish made of paper!
   ISBN 0-9704629-3-X

   1. cooperativeness--Juvenile fiction. 2. Friendship
 --Juvenile fiction. 3. Locomotives--Juvenile fiction.
 4. chocolate--Juvenile fiction. 5. Cookery (Chocolate)
 --Juvenile literature. [1. Cooperativeness--fiction.
 2. Friendship--Fiction. 3. Locomotives--fiction.
 4. chocolate--Fiction.] 1. Mason Rast, Barbara.
 II. Title.

   PZ7.K83746cH 2001   [E]
                   QB101-701033

The Chocolate Train

By Joanne Kornfeld

Illustrations by Barbara Mason Rast

EARTHKIDS PUBLISHING

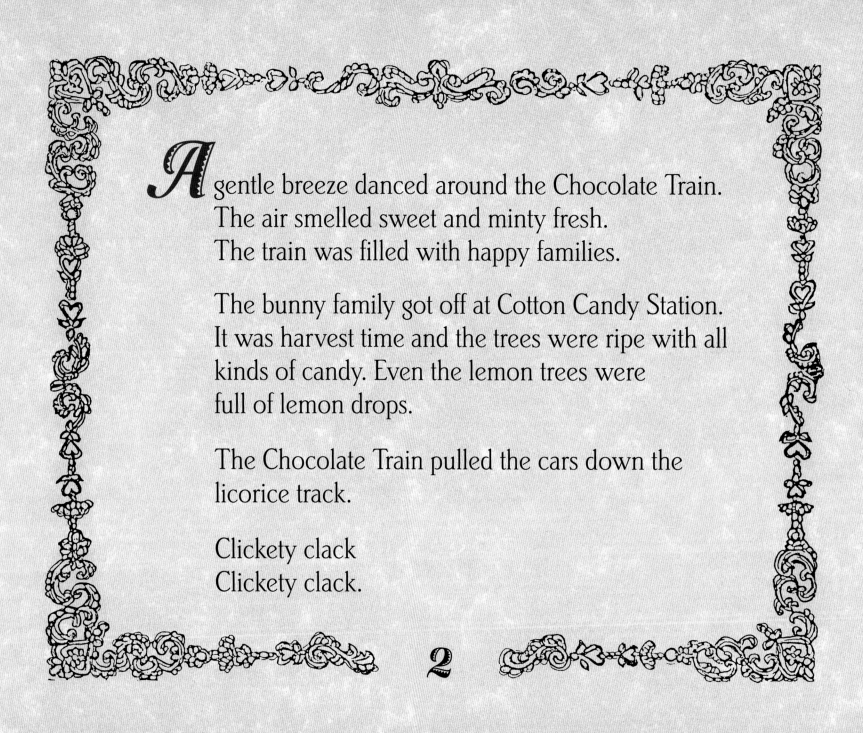

A gentle breeze danced around the Chocolate Train.
The air smelled sweet and minty fresh.
The train was filled with happy families.

The bunny family got off at Cotton Candy Station.
It was harvest time and the trees were ripe with all
kinds of candy. Even the lemon trees were
full of lemon drops.

The Chocolate Train pulled the cars down the
licorice track.

Clickety clack
Clickety clack.

2

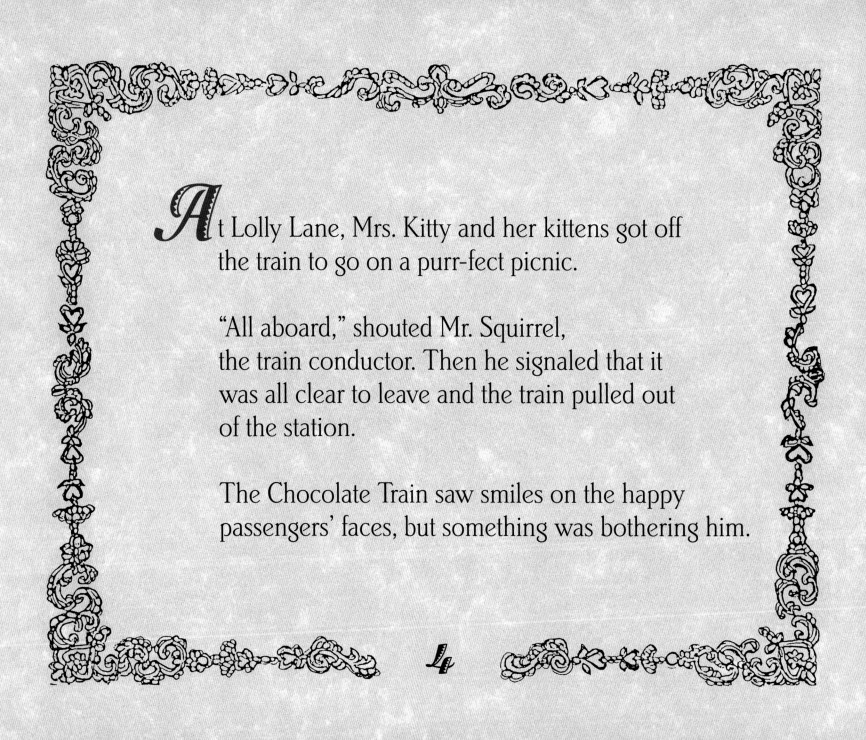

At Lolly Lane, Mrs. Kitty and her kittens got off the train to go on a purr-fect picnic.

"All aboard," shouted Mr. Squirrel, the train conductor. Then he signaled that it was all clear to leave and the train pulled out of the station.

The Chocolate Train saw smiles on the happy passengers' faces, but something was bothering him.

The Chocolate Train passed over the bridge at Gum Drop Gorge. It was one of his favorite places. The trees grew gift boxes. When the boxes were ripe, they would drop off the trees.

He saw the Mouse family taking a beautiful gift box home and he wondered what surprise the family would find inside.

The Chocolate Train suddenly wished that he could take a surprise box to his hometown friends too.

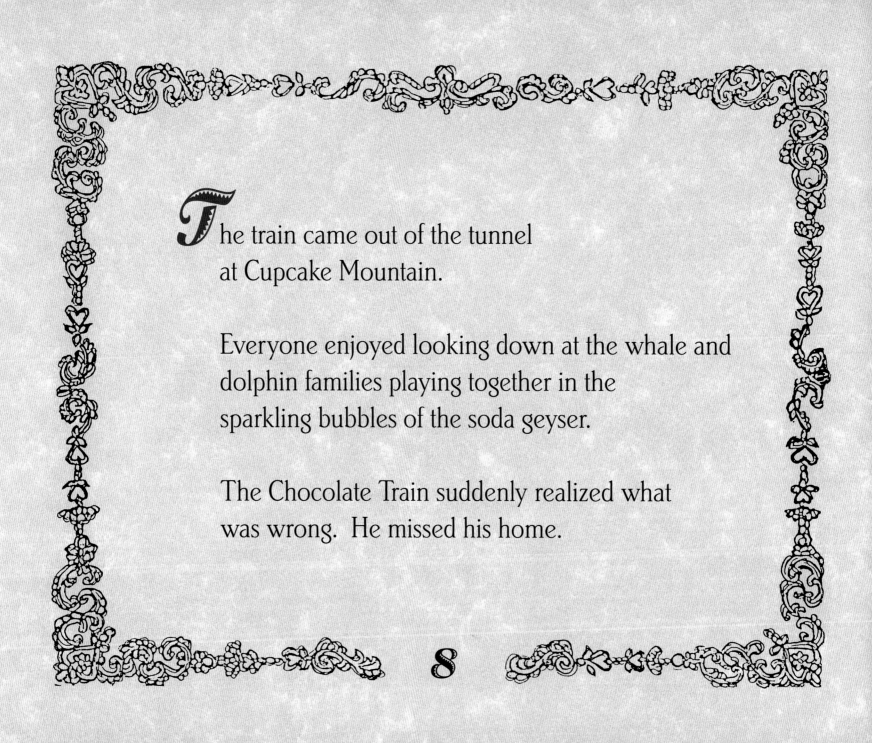

*T*he train came out of the tunnel
at Cupcake Mountain.

Everyone enjoyed looking down at the whale and
dolphin families playing together in the
sparkling bubbles of the soda geyser.

The Chocolate Train suddenly realized what
was wrong. He missed his home.

8

The Chocolate Train rested for a while at Marshmallow Marsh. He sighed as he looked at the delicious countryside.

"Why are you so sad?" asked Mr. Squirrel.

"I wish I could visit Chocolateville again. I miss my friends."

All the passengers loved the idea and were happy to cheer up their friend. When the train heard how kind they were, rainbow sparklers flew out of his smokestack, lighting up the sky.

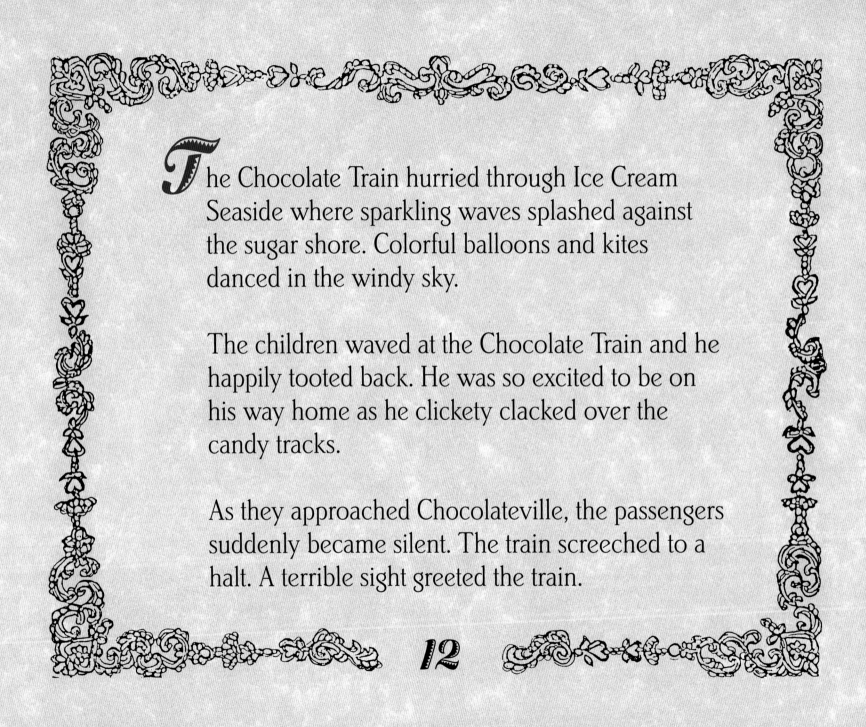

The Chocolate Train hurried through Ice Cream Seaside where sparkling waves splashed against the sugar shore. Colorful balloons and kites danced in the windy sky.

The children waved at the Chocolate Train and he happily tooted back. He was so excited to be on his way home as he clickety clacked over the candy tracks.

As they approached Chocolateville, the passengers suddenly became silent. The train screeched to a halt. A terrible sight greeted the train.

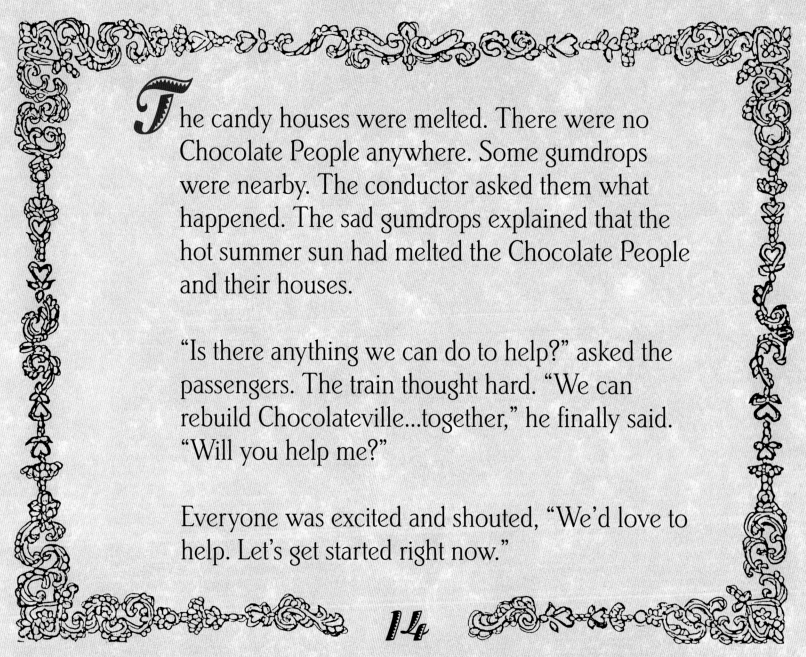

The candy houses were melted. There were no Chocolate People anywhere. Some gumdrops were nearby. The conductor asked them what happened. The sad gumdrops explained that the hot summer sun had melted the Chocolate People and their houses.

"Is there anything we can do to help?" asked the passengers. The train thought hard. "We can rebuild Chocolateville...together," he finally said. "Will you help me?"

Everyone was excited and shouted, "We'd love to help. Let's get started right now."

Dear Readers: You can help too. After reading this story, ask a GROWN UP to help you make your own chocolate candy and train candy dish using the directions at the back of this book.

The Gumdrops guided them to Chocolate Lake where the melted chocolate had flowed and slowly hardened. The children had fun scooping up the chocolate chunks from the lake. They gave the pieces to the parents to put in large hot vats.

Mr. Squirrel kindly warned the children NOT to go near the very HOT pots.

The parents poured the smooth melted chocolate into clean molds. Smiles emerged on the faces of the chocolate people. As the figures of the chocolate people formed in the molds, they were quickly wheeled into the icehouse to harden properly.

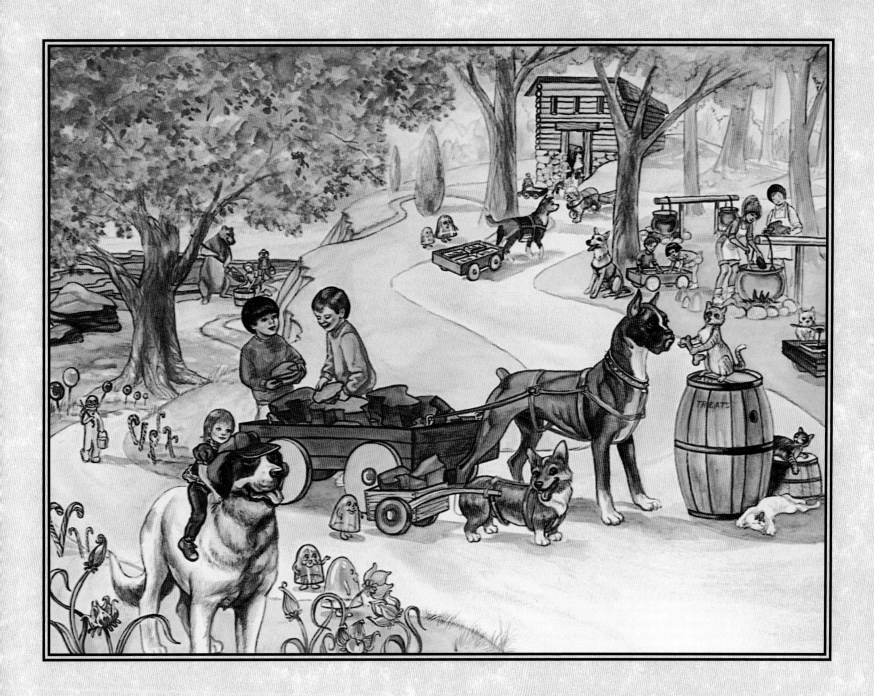

When the Chocolate People became solid, they popped out of their molds and gave chocolate kisses to everyone who had rescued them. Everyone was very happy that they had worked together to rebuild the town and help the Chocolate People.

The Chocolate Train loved being with his old...and new friends too.

As the cool evening sun was setting, the chocolate Train's happy heart was chugging and thumping...

Clickety clack
Clickety clack.

Making Chocolate Mold Candies With an Adult

DO NOT TRY THIS WITHOUT A GROWN-UP

Work in a cool kitchen for best results. Select directions for either Double Boiler, Crock Pot or Microwave method below.

Supplies

[Available in craft stores or specialty catalogs]

- ❑ 1 lb. Melting Chocolate Bits
- ❑ Candy or Lollipop Mold and Sticks
- ❑ Stirring Spoon
- ❑ Double Boiler, Crock Pot or Microwave Oven
- ❑ Colored Chocolate Bits- only for color painting variation
- ❑ 1 tsp. Vegetable Oil
- ❑ Pot Holders and heat-safe cookie sheet
- ❑ Microwave-safe bowl for microwave method

<u>Note</u>: Clean and dry everything thoroughly. Water drops will **ruin the shiny chocolate finish.**

Double Boiler Method

Fill 2/3 water in bottom pot and heat to simmer. Melt your chocolate bits on LOW heat in the TOP pot of your double boiler. Keep stirring so the mixture is creamy and not burnt.

Microwave Method

Melt chocolate bits in microwave-safe bowl for 30 seconds at half power and stop and stir. Repeat heating and stirring until all chocolate pieces are melted and creamy. Add up to 1 tsp. vegetable oil if mixture starts to become chunky and mix to a smooth consistency.

Crock Pot Method

Melt chocolate bits on lowest setting and stir until smooth and creamy. If mixture thickens, turn off pot, add up to 1 tsp. vegetable oil and mix to a smooth consistency.

When the Chocolate Mixture is Smooth and Creamy

1. PLAIN CANDY MOLDS: Carefully fill mold with melted mixture. Do not overfill.
   LOLLIPOP MOLDS: Submerge sticks deep into the mold so they will be firmly embedded when chocolate hardens.

2. Gently tap filled molds on the table to allow all air bubbles to escape.

3. Place the molds into the refrigerator for approximately 20-30 minutes. Do not allow the candy to turn frosty white.

4. Invert and gently tap out the SOLID chocolate. Wrap lollipops individually and keep chocolate cool and dry.

More Fun.........Painting Colors On Your Chocolate

For color on your chocolate, PREPAINT color on the inside of the mold BEFORE you fill it with the brown chocolate mixture.

Supplies: Pyrex dessert cups, a small narrow tip paint brush, a heating tray and pieces of colored chocolate.

1. Separate each color into a pyrex cup. Place cups on warm HEATING TRAY. Melt and stir colored chocolate pieces with your paint brush to keep chocolate creamy.

2. Working quickly, dip the paintbrush into the melted colored chocolate and paint inside your mold. (Example: red on a heart shape) Make sure the chocolate is solid before adding another color.

3. When all the colors are dry, fill up the rest of the mold with the brown liquid chocolate mixture.

4. Let chocolate settle and tap all air bubbles out.

5. Refrigerate until chocolate is solid and then gently pop out the candy.

Still More Fun.........Make the Chocolate Train Candy Dish

Use your imagination to decorate your candy dish and fill it up with your own homemade chocolate. Make some for your family and friends. Print names on the back of the Train Candy Dish for place settings at parties.

1. Trace, color and cut on the dark black lines of the model. Fold on the dotted lines. Secure the box with tape.

Hi! I make a great candy dish

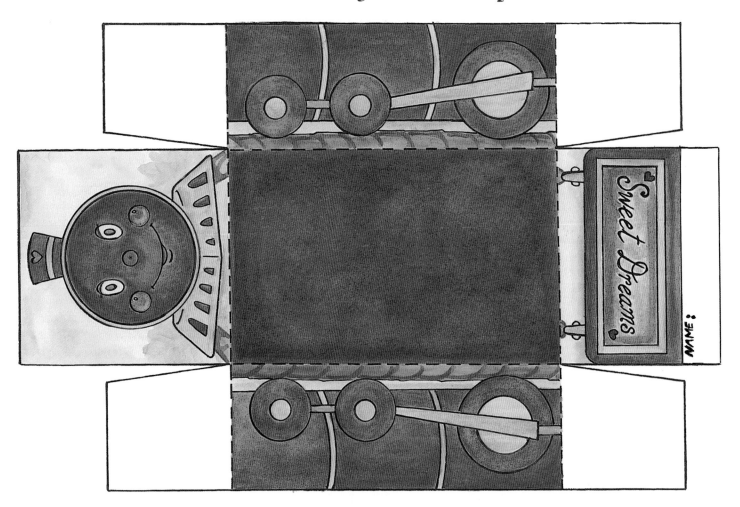

Instructions: 1. Trace me 3. Cut out on dark black outside lines.
2. Color me 4. Fold on dotted lines and secure with tape.

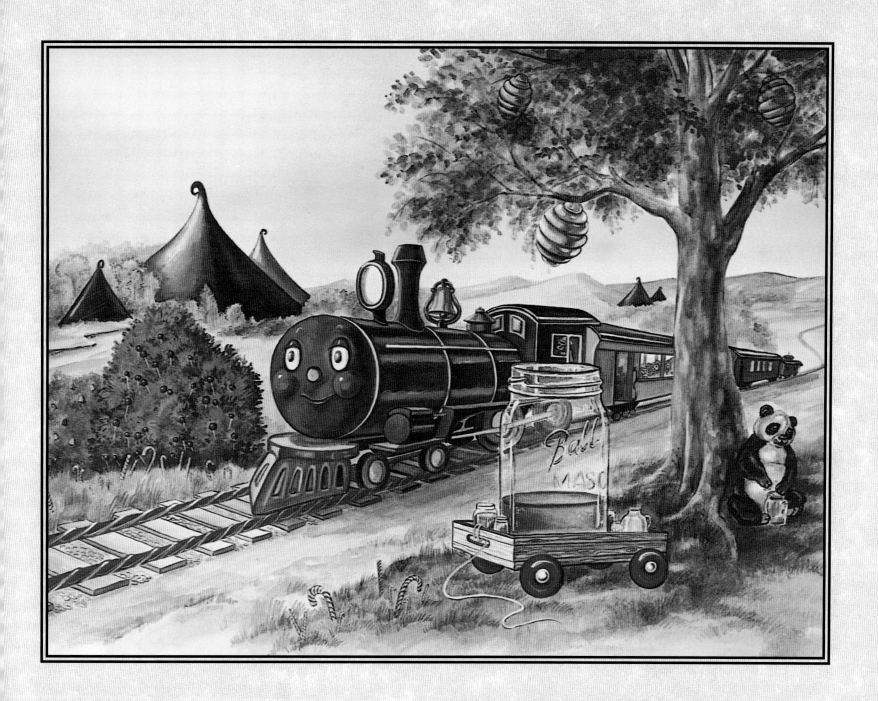

Say hello to the Chocolate Train @
www.earthkidspublishing.com

Order beautiful POSTERS from the "Chocolate Train" to hang
up in your child's room from our website.
They make wonderful gifts too.

See our other quality Books from Earthkids Publishing.

About the Author

Joanne Kornfeld holds a BA and MS in Education and has been a teacher for over 30
years. She was a contributing writer for Penny Pincher magazine. She composes
music, plays piano and violin, loves to paint and write stories. This book is a happy
reminder of the time she spent with her son and daughter making chocolate candies
after school and reading stories together at bedtime.

About the Illustrator

Barbara Mason Rast is a multi-faceted artist whose works include oil, watercolors,
pastels and airbrush. She is known for her portraits, murals, still life, realistic animals
(especially horses) and her illustrations for children. The work of Barbara Mason Rast
has been frequently displayed and is found in numerous private collections. Her first
illustrated book was <u>Rockster and the Giant Acorn</u>. She loves to create works of real-
ism and whimsical fantasy.

Many thanks to Marc Josloff for his invaluable contribution with this book's graphic design and
Lester Kornfeld for his excellent photographic support.